Flora's Tree House

Gabriel Alborozo

Henry Holt and Company ⟨ New York

Henry Holt and Company, *Publishers since 1866*
Henry Holt® is a registered trademark of Macmillan Publishing Group, LLC
175 Fifth Avenue, New York, NY 10010
mackids.com

Library of Congress Cataloging-in-Publication Data
Names: Alborozo, Gabriel, 1972–author, illustrator.
Title: Flora's tree house / Gabriel Alborozo.
Description: First edition. | New York : Henry Holt and Company, 2019. |
Summary: While Will has exciting adventures with aliens, mummies, and
more, his little sister, Flora, captures them in pictures to hang in her
tree house, making them even better than Will imagined.
Identifiers: LCCN 2018038290 | ISBN 9781627792264 (hardcover)
Subjects: | CYAC: Imagination—Fiction. | Drawing—Fiction. | Play—Fiction.
| Brothers and sisters—Fiction. | Tree houses—Fiction.
Classification: LCC PZ7.1.A43 Flo 2019 | DDC [E]—dc23
LC record available at https://lccn.loc.gov/2018038290

Our books may be purchased in bulk for promotional, educational, or business use. Please
contact your local bookseller or the Macmillan Corporate and Premium Sales Department at
(800) 221-7945 ext. 5442 or by email at MacmillanSpecialMarkets@macmillan.com.

First edition, 2019 / Designed by April Ward
The illustrations for this book were created digitally.
Printed in China by Toppan Leefung Printing Ltd., Dongguan City, Guangdong Province

1   3   5   7   9   10   8   6   4   2

For Mia and Elias
and brothers and sisters everywhere

"Pew! Pew!"

Flora's brother leaped from the tree and aimed his stick at her.
"Take that, alien menace!" shouted Will before racing across the field.
Flora watched as he zoomed off,
then opened her sketchbook. Will was a
good muse—but also a very loud one.

Flora finished sketching the aliens. She used an ultramarine blue crayon to color one alien and emerald green for the other.

"Hey, what are you drawing over there?" Will yelled.

"Nothing!" Flora replied. "Just keep doing what you're doing."

Once she was satisfied with her drawing, Flora
closed the sketchbook, packed up her supplies, and
climbed the ladder into her tree house.

Just as she finished hanging her new masterpiece, she received a very unwelcome visitor.

"Aha!" cried Will.

"Can't you read?" Flora replied.
Will's satisfaction at catching his sister off guard quickly
turned into a sense of awe.

"Wait a second . . .," he said.

"What **is** all of this?"

Flora was none too pleased with
her brother's intrusion. "This is my *private*
tree house, and I—"

NO
WILLS
ALLOWED!

"Are those the aliens I was just fighting?"
Will asked. He was always interrupting.
"Uh-huh," Flora answered.
"How did you know they
were blue and green?"

Before Flora could answer, Will raced to another drawing. "What's this one?"

"Don't you remember?" Flora asked. "You flew your rocket to Pluto.
But then it broke down, and you got very cold and hungry. So you
hitched a ride on a comet. You got home just in time for dinner."

"I do remember!" Will shivered
at the memory.

Will couldn't believe his little sister had drawn so many of his adventures. "What about this one?"

"That was the day you were a human cannonball! You flew the length of six fire trucks and set a new world record!"

"I did?" Will asked. Not only had his sister drawn his adventures, she'd made them even better.

Will walked over to another of his sister's masterpieces and leaned in close. "Hey, *you're* in this one!"

"It looked like you needed some help," Flora said. "The dragon had already gobbled up your mates, so while you distracted him, I raced into his cave and gathered the treasure."

Flora couldn't remember the last time she had had so much fun with Will. She pulled another drawing from the wall. "I think this was my most favorite adventure ever."

Will peered at the picture.

"Hey! Why aren't I in this one?" he asked.

"You're not the only one who has adventures, you know," explained Flora. "Besides, I think you had to go to the dentist that day."

"But you *were* with me when I went to Peru!" said Flora, showing a different picture.

"Whoa!" said Will. "Are those man-eating plants?"

Flora grinned. "Yup!"

"And an escape elephant?"
Will gasped. "That's so awesome!"

Flora quickly grabbed another picture.

"What about when you found the pharaoh's tomb, and all the mummies came to life? That was pretty major!"

Will looked very hard at the picture. "How did you know? Wait! Is that you?"

Flora chuckled as
Will gave her a wink.
"I thought one of those
mummies looked familiar!"
Will pointed toward another
of his sister's drawings.

"I wish you had been with me when I dug that tunnel to Australia," Will said. "It was really hard work."

Flora smiled. "Me too." Though he could be loud and annoying, Will did have a pretty good imagination. She sat down next to her brother and opened her sketchbook to a fresh page.

Suddenly, she stood and clutched his arm.
"Did you feel that?" she whispered.

"The tree house is sailing away!"
Will stood and held her hand. "We need
to be careful of pirates, Flora. Hold on!"